BEING BULLIED

First edition for the United States, Canada,
and the Philippines published 1991
by Barron's Educational Series, Inc.

Design David West Children's Book Design

All inquiries should be addressed to:
Barron's Educational Series, Inc.
250 Wireless Boulevard
Hauppauge, NY 11788

International Standard Book No. 0-8120-4661-7

Library of Congress Catalog Card No. 91-14192

Library of Congress Cataloging-in Publication Data

Petty, Kate.
    Being Bullied / Kate Petty : illustrations by Charlotte Firmin.
        p.   cm. -- (Playgrounds)
    Summary: Rita is bullied by another girl at school but finds
relief when she stands up to her.
    ISBN 0-8120-4661-7
    (1. Bullies--Fiction. 2. Schools--Fiction) I. Firmin,
Charlotte, ill. II. Title. III. Series: Petty, Kate. Playgrounds.
PZ7.P44814Bc   1991
(E)--dc20   91-14192   CIP   AC

Printed in Belgium
1234   987654321

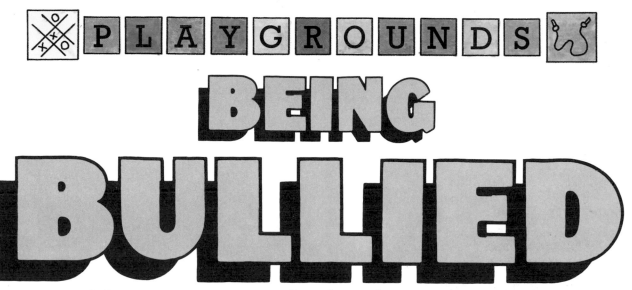

PLAYGROUNDS
BEING
BULLIED

Kate Petty and Charlotte Firmin

Barron's
New York • Toronto

Rita doesn't want to go to school today.
"Come on, Rita, put your shoes on."

Rita takes as long as she can.

"Cheer up," says Mom as she hugs Rita
goodbye.
"I think she misses her friend Alice,"
says Miss Wood.

"But I'm afraid Alice won't be back
in school for a few days."

Rita has to sit next to Bella
while Alice is away.
When Rita draws a spider,
Bella pushes her arm.

"Never mind," says Miss Wood.
"Turn your paper over and try again."
By the time Rita has found her pencil,
Bella has made a big scribble
on Rita's blank paper.

Rita thinks Bella is a pest.
"Bella scribbled on my paper,"
Rita tells the teacher.

Bella thinks Rita is a tattletale.

In the playground, Bella and her friends
call Rita names.

"You'd better not go telling tales again..."

Rita wonders what Bella will do.

"How was school today?"
Mom gives Rita something to drink.
"OK," says Rita,

and goes to watch TV.

"How was school today?"
Dad tucks Rita into bed.
"OK," says Rita,

and hides under the covers.

The next day, Bella spills Rita's paint,
draws all over her work, steps on her toes,
pushes in front of her in the line,
and hides her lunchbox.

Rita doesn't tell anybody.

After school, Rita is very quiet.

"How was school today?"
Mom makes a snack for her.
"OK," says Rita.
"It wasn't," says Mom. "I can tell."
So, finally, Rita tells Mom about Bella.

"Bella is a bully and she must be stopped.
Don't let her scare you," says Mom.
"I'll take you to school early and
we'll talk to Miss Wood together.
But, don't worry — I won't say anything
you don't want me to."

Mom tells Miss Wood about Bella. Miss Wood
promises to keep an eye on her.

Bella is an angel all morning.

Rita sees that sometimes Bella can be nice.

She even gives Rita one of her stickers.

But, during recess, while Miss Wood
isn't watching, Bella and her friends
tease Rita and call her names —
"Sneak." "Tattletale." "Baby."
"You don't scare me," says Rita.

Rita makes sure she's with other
children when Miss Wood isn't around.
She tries not to pay attention to Bella.

Bella finds it isn't much fun teasing Rita
when Rita doesn't seem to mind. Suddenly,
Rita isn't afraid of Bella anymore.

Alice is back in school. Rita is happy
to be with her friend again.
"Bella has big brothers and sisters,"
says Alice. "They bully her at home."
Bella does push people around a lot.
But Rita knows that she can be friendly.
Bella sometimes even shares her things.

Rita is glad she told Mom
when she was bullied at school.

THINGS TO DO...

Draw a picture of Rita and Bella at school.
Or draw a picture of yourself at school.

Talk about how Rita felt when Bella picked
on her.
Or talk about why you think Bella is a bully.
Or talk about a time when you were unhappy
in the playground.

Make up a play or use puppets to tell the
story in the book.
Or make up a play about something that happened
in your playground.

Remember what to do if someone is bullying
you. Tell a grown-up. Try not to let the bully
upset you. Stay with other people.

PRINTED IN BELGIUM BY

proost

INTERNATIONAL BOOK PRODUCTION